LISA MORTON'S

WEIRD WOMEN AND OTHER ANOMALIES

WHEN I WAS 15, I SIMULTANEOUSLY DISCOVERED BOTH WEIRD FICTION AND USED BOOKSTORES. I RECALL THE SPECIFIC AGE BECAUSE IT WAS A YEAR AFTER MY PARENTS DIVORCED AND I WAS LIVING WITH MY MOM.

We didn't have much money; mom refused—against, of course, both the advice of her attorney and prevailing wisdom—to take any alimony, saying that she could make her own living. I made some spending money from being an amateur magician (I did a lot of kids' birthday parties), although I was as likely to have book money from foregoing lunch at school and saving those few cents for books instead. Who cared about a little hunger when there were books to devour?

We were living in San Diego at the time, and I discovered a used paperback book store in El Cajon (although I also got Mom to occasionally drive me to the late, great Wahrenbrock's and Adams Avenue Bookstore). For fifty cents each, I could load up on paperbacks. I was soon moving past the classics I'd already gorged myself on as I discovered Robert E. Howard (thanks in no small part to the Frank Frazetta covers), H. P. Lovecraft, and more.

I loved them. I thrilled to Conan's muscular adventures. My youthful brain was blown by Lovecraft's cosmic horrors (although even as a kid I recall reading "The Horror at Red Hook" and being disturbed by the racist overtones). Clark Ashton Smith's visions of fantastical worlds left me dreaming.

One thing, though, made me begin to turn away from these tales, and it was this: there was seldom anyone like me in these books. By "like me", I mean a female protagonist who wasn't a hero's love interest or a terrifying demigod's victim.

I'm guessing I wasn't the only girl who wanted a piece of the sword-swinging, monster-bashing, eldritch god-invoking pie. My fantasies never once involved fainting at the feet of some serpentine abomination while a mighty male carved a trail of carnage to set me free. Somehow I never imagined myself being tied to an altar while a whey-faced priest summoned something to eat me...or worse. I grew up with The Avengers on the telly, watching Mrs. Peel dispatch bad guys while Steed poured champagne; was it so much to ask to find just a little of that in my fiction?

Apparently it was, because with the very, very occasional delight like the Aquilonian pirate Valeria in Howard's "Red Nails", there were few interesting women to be found in early weird fiction. Even antagonists were rare; note that Lovecraft's "The Thing on the Doorstep", featuring the villainess Asenath Waite Derby, was described (accurately) by Peter Cannon as being "the only Lovecraft story with a strong or important female character."

3

Jump on board and take an extraordinary trip in **WEIRD WOMEN AND OTHER ANOMALIES**—an all-lady lineup of visionary authors that will challenge your perceptions and expand your horizons in **FORBIDDEN FUTURES 3!**

ARTIST: MIKE DUBISCH **PUBLISHER:** ODDNESS **EDITOR:** CODY GOODFELLOW

WHEN I WAS 15, I SIMULTANEOUSLY DISCOVERED BOTH WEIRD FICTION AND USED BOOKSTORES. I RECALL THE SPECIFIC AGE BECAUSE IT WAS A YEAR AFTER MY PARENTS DIVORCED AND I WAS LIVING WITH MY MOM.

One might suppose that part of the problem is that very few women were publishing weird fantasy, but here's where we open the portal and step into an alternate world: a surprising number of female writers were published in the nascent years of weird fiction, just as many more women wrote ghost stories in the nineteenth century than most of us realize. One overview of Weird Tales, for example, estimates that about 17% of its authors were female; sometimes they wrote under initials (C. L. Moore is surely the most famous example of this), and sometimes they bore names that…well, sounded likelier to be masculine (Bassett Morgan). The most extraordinary of the female contributors to Weird Tales during its heyday must be Allison V. Harding: with 36 Weird Tales stories to her credit, she was ahead of contributors like Ray Bradbury and Frank Belknap Long. She produced one character, "The Damp Man", who proved so popular with readers that she wrote two sequels. Yet Harding has vanished into obscurity, leaving behind much speculation about who she was: an attorney named Jean Milligan, who didn't want to be associated with the pulps? The wife of a man named Lamont Buchanan, who worked for Weird Tales and may have been the actual author? Or was it some sort of "house name" like Ellery Queen?

Or take Amelia Reynolds Long, a prolific author who wrote in multiple genres. Long's 1930 Weird Tales contribution "The Thought Monster" was filmed in 1958 as Fiend Without a Face (whose animated brains-dragging-spinal columns are the stuff of legend in my house). Long's weird fiction has never been collected.

Mary Elizabeth Counselman was second only to Harding in the number of stories published in Weird Tales (30 in total); her 1930 story "The Three Marked Pennies" is considered to be one of the most popular stories to have appeared in the magazine. Counselman's fiction, at least, was collected…once, in the 1964 British paperback Half in Shadow (later reprinted in hardback by Arkham House).

Some of the answer seems to be that these women simply didn't want to be found. They wrote under

SO WHAT HAPPENED HERE? WHY ARE THESE WOMEN LARGELY CONSIGNED TO HISTORICAL DISCUSSIONS AND FOUND ONLY IN MOLDERING COPIES OF PULP MAGAZINES WHILE THEIR MALE COUNTERPARTS CONTINUE TO BE REPRINTED AND READ?

initials and pseudonyms to disguise their writing interests from employers; they didn't attend conventions, they didn't write letters to their male colleagues, and they obviously didn't have social media. They all had other jobs—they were attorneys, teachers, and librarians.

Since they didn't care about literary fame and probably didn't need the writing paychecks to survive, why did they do it?

There's only one answer: they loved it. They all possessed the peculiar gifts for writing weird fiction, and they relished any chance to put those gifts to use to entertain readers.

Which brings us to 2019, and this magazine.

Fortunately, things have changed in the last eighty or so years. Sure, some women still use initials, and they still can't live on what they make as writers…but they can now promote themselves, they go to public events right alongside their male writer friends, and they have their own books out there. Women in weird fantasy and horror are even celebrated now, with themed anthologies, an entire month (yes, one whole month!)dedicated to them, and magazines like this one daring to offer up all-female rosters.

Sure, there are still a few Damp Men crouched in corners of dank basements (usually in their parents' houses), feverishly tapping out their messages that "Women are too delicate to write horror." Well, to that endangered species whose extinction no one will lament I say…

Fuck that shit.

Now turn the page and read some great fiction from writers who love what they do, and who just happen to be women.

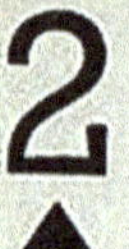

KNOW YOUR ENEMY
UNCLE KRUST'S
GUIDE TO MEN
★ ★ ★
SPOTTER CARDS
★ ★ ★
FORBIDDEN FUTURES
PORTLAND, U. S. A.

2 ♠ — BOG LURKER

2
♠
BOG LURKER
—Hates to masturbate alone.
—Mistakes all other living things for
   inhibited, overly fastidious Bog Lurkers.
—Only known organism that can satisfy all
   nutritional needs with own excrement.
—Is really sorry if you're offended.
♠
2

J
♠
GARGOYLE
—Reproduces by impregnating Face-
   book profiles.
—He's not ugly, you're just shallow.
—Are these compliments and/or favors
   viable sexual currency?
—Is gonna tell everybody you did, anyway,
   so you might as well...
♠
J

6
♣
EDGELORD
—Has tattoo commemorating Pizzagate;
   not so sure about Holocaust.
—Cleaned his room, so you should totally
   blow him. It's science.
—Voluntarily celibate to deny you sex.
—All triggers, no bullets.
♣
6

10 ♦ — TECHNOCRAT

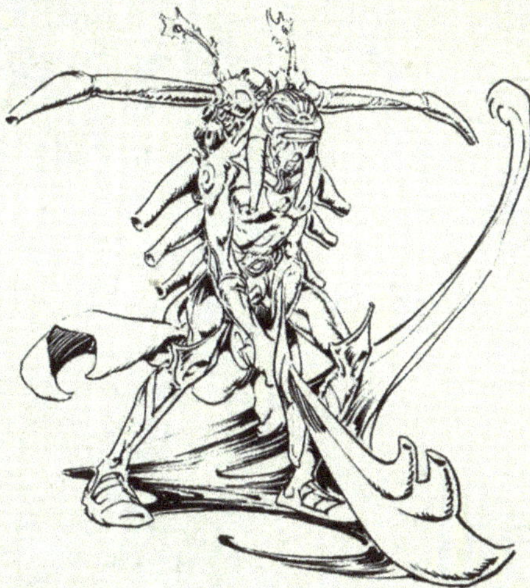

- Most dates on Fortnite; lowest kill ratio on OKCupid.
- Demographically identical to you; totally not stalking you.
- Is building a better version of you in his parents' basement.
- Better versions of him drown in the shower every day.

A ♦ — KENNY ROGERS

- Knows when to hold, when to fold.
- Knows when to walk away, when to run.
- Never counts money when sitting at table.
- Remembers to tell you he's poly before you find out he's married.

A ♥ — SUPER-ALLY

- Traveled back in time to kill baby Hitler while you were reading this, but he was really, really cute.
- Weaponized empathy.
- Super-listening skills let him hear anyone being wrong on the Internet.
- Secretly at least two other male types in this deck, but heroically suppressing it.

K ♣ — BRAINATOR

- Uses powers of invincible logic to reverse irritating laws of biology, physics, history.
- Can instantly calculate and discard all possible outcomes of being "nice" in any situation.
- Can transform into anything; can't change his mind about anything.
- We're all living in a flawed simulation he's running to prepare to go on a date.

DAISYCO
CAPTURE MEMORIES!
WITH DAISYCO HOLOGRAM TAPES
FORBIDDEN FUTURES 8

ALWAYS A BRIDE

JESSICA McHUGH

THE HOUSE BLUSHES.

From the sleek steel foundation to the hemispheric roof, the AtomiClass DaisyPod-4 glows hot pink when Molly's taxi docks at the compound. The newly erected residential pods shone like textbook acne from the air—bulgy domes with the angry tinge of infection under the Mars sunset—but despite their rosy uniformity, Molly knew which pod was hers.

And it knows her.

It's the smallest model— "an economic love-nest" according to the AtomiClass adverts, and "the ideal honeymoon hideaway." The description is accurate enough from the outside, but Molly supposes she won't know for sure until Robert joins her. For now, she settles for his hologram.

He's pacing a hotel room on Earth, his image broken and fuzzy as it flits around the DaisyPod like a honeybee in an arboretum. Molly hasn't even taken off her shoes and she feels like she needs a nap. She twists her engagement ring, her skin still inflamed and itchy despite the decades-old callus around the finger.

"Robert, please stand still. I'm getting dizzy."

"Sorry, babe, I'm already late for the keynote speaker, and I still need to shave."

"You look fine to me."

He stops briefly to throw her a kiss. It was an adorable quirk when they were dating, but he doesn't even look at her anymore. He spits the kiss into his fist and lobs it like a carnival baseball, focused more on speed than accuracy.

She catches the gesture anyway, holding it to her chest as she says, "I miss you."

He messes up knotting his tie and growls in frustration as he rips it from his neck. "I gotta go, babe. Do you need anything else from me?"

If she could articulate everything she needed, she wouldn't be alone in a DaisyPod, talking to his hologram. She spins her engagement ring, and endorphins flood her brain. Better than drugs, better than any man or woman who might've been the one if not for the ring she refused to remove when she and Robert were apart.

But she could never tell him any of this. So she shakes her head, and his image shudders before blinking out.

He doesn't say "I love you."

She doesn't say "I love you."

The house says, "*I'm afraid I've lost the connection.*"

THE HOUSE'S VOICE IS SLIGHTLY LOWER THAN MOLLY'S, WITH A LILT THAT'S MORE AFFECTATION THAN ACCENT.

It comes at her from all sides, but it's loudest in the foyer, where blue light pulses under the closet door. Behind it, within the recessed chamber, an android sleeps, the light in its sleek barrel chest a steady blue beam and its face devoid of detail. A sign above the robot reads, "*Hello, I'm Daisy. Greet To Activate,*" but Molly clamps her lips in worry.

ADVENTURE AWAITS!
ACTIVATE YOUR DAISY TODAY
DAISYCO

She'd read the catalog front to back, back to front, the lovely euphemisms like a white sheets covering a corpse, as well as the autopsied truth outlining the intentions of the house and its android guide. But nothing had prepared her for something so...clunky. Daisy looks more like a bludgeon than a flower, and Molly's heart sinks to her stomach.

Maybe she made a mistake with the DaisyPod –4. Maybe she isn't ready for this.

She expects the android to be cold, but when Molly presses her hand to Daisy's chest, warmth pulses into her fingertips, and the sign overhead glows red.

With a stomach loosening sigh, she says, "Hello, Daisy," and jumps back as the android starts vibrating wildly in the wall.

As bands of color surge through its hull, the bludgeon softens. Its skull shifts to a delicate collection of mountains and valleys, and two opal eyes flutter into holographic existence, glittering in the hollows while neon blue lips dance over a sculpted mouth.

"*Hello again, Molly.*"

Daisy smiles, and with a troubling "pop!" the glowing sign spews a handful of sparks and fizzles out. The android's body abruptly dislodges from the chamber, and Daisy falls forward like a dead tree. Molly yelps as she and the robot fall to the floor like children in an orchestra pit, all smack and clang as they flounder for footing.

"What the hell was that?" Molly frees herself from tangled metal limbs and works herself to a standing position. She expects the robot to be right behind her, but Daisy's still on the floor, rocking like an overturned turtle.

"What's wrong? Can't you walk?"

Daisy's limbs crumple inward and her voice shrinks to hushed but melodic breath. "*I'm sorry, Molly, but you need to teach me.*"

"What? I don't remember anything about that in the catalog."

"*Article 54–A regarding genetic linking to lease-holder: Some hands-on instruction required.*"

"What does that mean?"

"*It means I need you to teach me.*"

Molly's exhausted all of a sudden. Her hip is aching more than usual thanks to the fall, and she wants it to end. All of it. No more waiting. No more euphemistic games. She wants the supposed "honeymoon hideaway" to do its job.

The lonely bride looks to the living room like Robert might still be there, fighting with his Victoria knot, and Daisy emits a sentimental hum.

"*I can bring him back if you want. Or anyone. Whenever you miss them.*"

"They aren't real."

"*No, they aren't real. Would you like something real?*"

She nods, and the android's trunk shifts as if it's being moved by an army of ants. It twists and bends until Daisy's sitting up, her smooth silver legs extended, arms limp at her sides, and several pieces of thin flexible metal slowly emerging from her ankles and wrists.

"*I need you to teach me, Molly.*"

"I'm not strong enough to carry you."

"*I was made for you to carry.*" Her blue light beats fast. "*I'm real, Molly. And my needing you is real.*"

Tears rise in Molly's eyes, and the breath drains from her lungs. She holds her chest as she sinks to the floor beside the android, whose holographic lips downturn in worry.

"*Are you all right?*"

She doesn't know how to answer. No, she isn't all right, because despite living on her own for the last four decades, being alone in this pod doesn't feel like the cramped studios and moldy basement apartments of her younger days. Not even her later years living in Glaxxes motel zoos, being watched day and night by wealthy voyeurs, made her feel as small and exposed as she does right now. Nothing in her life had prepared her to be needed. Not Robert when he was around, not Peter, Tom, or Genevieve, or the multitude of eyes she pretended not to see outside her Glaxxes zoo window. They didn't need her, but they wanted her, and being wanted— even fleetingly—was better than nothing. But not forever.

Gazing at the android that requires her instruction to function, Molly pushes that long-ago lesson into the dark with Tom and Gen and the others, and nods at Daisy. Yes, she *is* all right, better than all right, and as she lifts her bare wrists to the robot, the thin buckles open and stretch to close around her.

Cuffed around her arms and legs, her waist and neck, Daisy and Molly move as one, every flex and extension a priceless education. It's awkward at first; they are toddler and toy, tripping over and carrying each other from room to room in strange giddy fogs, and Molly soon loses track of where she ends and Daisy begins. They are seamlessly hinged, each step recorded in both of their bones as they bound around the pod. Time folds and reshapes them, and it is always daytime in the DaisyPod–4, so Molly keeps walking and leaping and, for the first time in

SAFARI EUROPA

in a AtomiClass DaisyPod-4

a long time, weeping when she finds herself in the bathroom.

It's so clean it feels like a threat. The sink looks naked without toppled prescription bottles and toothpaste tubes curled up like dead worms. Molly prefers clutter; it comforts her to see everything she owns scattered out before her, always identifiable, always available. Whether a current necessity or scrap of the past, she delights in being able to put her finger on an object and remember precisely why it kept her alive.

"*Your heart is racing.*"

"I'll be fine."

"*It's faster now. You're frightened.*"

"I said I'm fine."

"*Now you're angry.*"

When she stamps her foot, Daisy stamps with her, and the bathroom shakes all around them. The clean veneer blurs like it was just a projection, and in the static, Molly sees her pill bottles, her razors and bobby pins and the tubes of neon lipstick she was never courageous enough to wear in public.

The overhead lights switch off, and the mirrors are suddenly transparent—for Molly, at least. The woman on the other side doesn't see her and keeps right on squeezing grease out of her pores and scraping plaque from her teeth. The bald bulbs over the other woman's mirror hang like elderly testicles, casting their dim lights directly into the orange bottles and making lighthouses of them all. They shine on the woman, but Molly looks beyond her to the zoo windows. The crowd is massive. They struggle to get a good spot, packed in like spastic sardines, but Robert is serene at the smudged glass. When the splotchy-faced woman looks over her shoulder, he throws her a kiss and massages his groin when she catches it.

She'll still holding his kiss in one withered fist when she turns back to the mirror and looks Molly dead in the eyes. Both women lean in, both women touch the mirror. Only one smiles at what she sees.

The lights flip back on, and Molly's breath fogs up her reflection. In that moment, she knows she made the right choice. The exhaustion that rolled her like a vindictive ocean wave is a seashell now. It's been scrubbed of its sharp edges, now soft and pink as a spring morning on Earth, whispering of its years in bondage. She feels light, like bubbles rising in a champagne flute.

"*I'm walking, Molly! I'm walking just like you!*"

She hadn't noticed the android's disconnection, but it's standing on its own now, chin lifted, chest puffed, and blue lips curled into a satisfied bow as she demonstrates the stride she'd learned. But Molly hadn't walked so confidently outside the pod. She had to hunch in her basement apartments and often felt like she was slithering when she crossed her room at the zoo.

Following Daisy's proud stride, she finds herself falling into the same rhythm. Her chin is indeed lifted and her sternum raised to the heavens. She imagines her own pulsing blue light at her breast as they march round and round, laughing and singing as the cameras whir in pursuit.

A prolonged honk halts Molly, and Daisy slams into her back. Apologizing, the android shakes off the collision and hurries to the door. It opens automatically, and Daisy greets the delivery man with a more robotic voice than she'd been using with Molly. When he thrusts out a clipboard, the tip of Daisy's right pinkie finger flips open and a pen pops out. She signs the pad, and he thanks her.

"*Thank you. Have an AtomiClassy day.*"

"What is it?" Molly asks, craning to see around the door.

Daisy beckons her outside to the small but lustrous two-seater spacecab in the driveway. It looks exactly like the pod, right down to its sunset hue, and as Molly joins Daisy's side she realizes the android skin has turned the same color.

"It's all connected," Molly says, amazed. "You, the house, the car..."

"*And you, Molly.*" Daisy blinks her large opal eyes. "*Do you want to take a drive?*"

"I don't know how."

Smiling, the android opens the hatch to the driver's seat. "*Let me teach you.*" It helps her in, and she twists her engagement ring as the android goes limp on the driveway and the cab flares with life.

It's simple transferring the DaisyPod–4's consciousness to the cab, but Molly's transference is another matter entirely. She didn't think she'd set foot outside the compound again, so the prospect of being back in the world that repeatedly used her up and discarded her doesn't exactly excite her. But then the cab's engine rumbles to life, and Daisy's voice purring from the steering wheel vibrates her hands, comforting as the holographic clutter that clogs up the ship's dashboard. Fast food cups and bank receipts, cheap knick-knacks and dead bugs: all the garbage she'd let pile up if she'd owned a ship allows her to relax into the seat and enjoy the journey.

Her hands are on the wheel, but she doesn't steer. It's all Daisy, carrying them from the compound to the frenetic streets downtown, turning and halting at the cherry red traffic bulbs freckled between

FORBIDDEN FUTURES 4
LIVE THE MOST
DANGEROUS GAME
ON TITAN!
DAISUCO
14

the ***buildings.*** The cabs and spaceships buzzing through the airspace look like bubbles in the glossy architecture, each spire and hemispheric structure also distorting the reflections of pedestrians on moving walkways.

She watches them the way she was watched. Eyes fixed and widening. Tongue curled against the roof of her mouth then unrolling like an old rug concealing a corpse. Fingers wanting to wander and clench and strangle and two words longing to smash the barriers to bits.

"SEE ME."

There are a fleet of ships ahead, each one a beauty. With sparkle and roar, they make her promises that Molly wishes they'd keep. They barrel ahead, boisterous as young love, and she closes her eyes, wondering how the downtown mountains will change her reflection.

Her seat belt tightens, and the cab fills with warmth. It feels like Daisy is hugging her from behind, or like they might still be attached. That feeling of heaviness is a hallelujah that encircles Molly like a vow. The spacecraft zooms down the street, and the ancient callus on Molly's ring finger itches so bad she rubs it against the steering wheel.

"I thought you wanted something meaningful."

"Yes."

"No one has been good to you. No one has known you. I know you, Molly. I've been you, and you've been me."

The spacecraft cuts around a training cab and into a steady flow of evening commuters.

Daisy's voice vibrates in her fingers. *"I won't leave you. We're in this together. I was made for you to carry."*

"I don't know how, Daisy. I'm afraid."

"Stay with me, Molly. I'll teach you."

The itch is overwhelming. With a grunt, Molly spins her engagement ring, and the spacecraft rolls like a boulder through oncoming traffic.

BLUE LIGHT PULSES FAINTLY IN THE DARK.

There's a ring on her finger. On every finger. On her wrists and ankles and around her waist. So many promises, so many plans. So many fat eyes outside thin windows keeping her small, hunched, and slithering, yet so few who wished to see her any other way. Watching her strut so confident through the pod would've disgusted them. Seeing her glad to teach and open to learn would've sent them running in opposite directions. But they're all dead now—they must be— the crash was so bad.

Molly feels weightless, yet there's a distinct feeling of compression that keeps her serene as bleeding colors join the flashing blue. She calls out for Daisy, but her friend doesn't come. She shouts for help, but not even an echo replies.

The bathroom light is on, magnifying the torturous cleanliness, but as soon as she concentrates on how much she hates it, a layer of flickering clutter fills the vanity, the floor, and every corner of the DaisyPod–4. As sweet as it is, she can't help imagining all the lovers who would've hated it. God knows where Robert actually is these days, but she wants to make him see her here, commanding the fabric of space-time.

"Daisy, connect me with Robert Mayer."

No response.

"Daisy, open an inter-dimensional line to Robert Mayer."

Silence.

The lights go out in the bathroom, and Molly can see the woman in the transparent mirror again. She was never so shiny when she was in the Glaxxes zoo, and her face was never so interesting. With smooth panels of metal and broken bone shards making a futuristic castle of her skull, both Molly and her former self earn scores of glistening stares from the voyeurs outside. Robert is there, still salivating, this time on bended knee, and Peter is pawing the glass. Genevieve has already left with a younger girl, and Trey is mocking her despite the roses in his hands.

Molly reaches out, grasping for every person she loved her over the last sixty years, everyone who left her always a bride, never a wife, but the metallic pens that tip her fingers clack on the mirror and keep her past forever at a distance.

She draws back, then taps the mirror again, playfully.

It's real. And it's just a reflection. No one on the other side can touch her anymore—not even herself. It's just another piece of glass, another wall of broken promises. Even if they can somehow find a way through the barrier, they're harmless to something as special as her.

A strange and lovely android lifts her head, curls her neon lips, and walks through her holographic clutter to the chamber in the wall. She will have forgotten how to walk by the time she wakes again, but she will have forgotten everything else too. And everyone. Every twist of the ring.

Her frame locks into place, the sign glows hot pink, and the house blushes.

"Hello, I'm Molly. Greet To Activate."

A JUDGMENT MADE CAN NEVER BEND

MOLLY TANZER

"Cat people, like Babycakes?"

"What is Babycakes?"

Sam was astonished. "Neely Comics? Superdeluxe-dot-com?" The utter lack of recognition on her co-worker's face surprised her. "He did that song about George Washington having like twenty goddamn dicks?" Still nothing. "Did you never experience the wonder that was *Wizard People, Dear Reader*?"

"I don't think so. What is it?"

"It's an alternative soundtrack to the first Harry Potter film… sort of like a book on tape, but it synchs up, mostly, to the film?" They'd gotten away from the point. "Anyway, so no? Cat people like… Bowie? Or the film? *Films*?" Sam was pretty sure the one from the '80s was a remake.

"David Bowie was in a film called *Cat People*?"

Sam shook her head. "So which cat people?"

"What do you mean?"

Jeff was a co-worker. Fate had assigned Sam and him to the same line on the same schedule at the factory where they worked assembling medical devices. There did their commonalities end. Usually they did not speak, but that day, Sam had forgotten her book.

"What do you mean what do I mean?" Sam asked. "*You* asked *me* if I knew anything about cat people!"

"I just didn't realize there were so many of them," he said. Sam blinked. "Billy made it seem like some huge secret."

Sam had been on the knife's edge of returning to work early to get away from this conversation, but Jeff drew her back in with surprising—and likely unintentional—deftness.

"Who is Billy?"

"Billy's my buddy. He works in a grow."

"And he says there are cat people?"

Jeff nodded solemnly.

"Where?"

"Rocky Flats."

Sam should have guessed the decommissioned nuclear weapons production facility would tie into this somehow. In Colorado, weird stories were destined to be set there, or at Denver International Airport. "Rocky Flats has been a wildlife refuge since 2007," she said calmly. "Nothing more. And they just opened up the trails to the public for hiking and stuff. If there were mutant cat people living there or whatever, I doubt they would have done that."

A look of triumph came into Jeff's eyes. "Billy says there's over six hundred acres that aren't open to the public, and that's where the cat people are."

"And how does Billy know this?"

"He saw them when he was fishing."

If Billy was eating the fish from Rocky Flats, no wonder he was seeing things. "What were the cat people doing?" she asked.

"He just said they were there and he saw them. They had spears, and were hunting in a pack."

Sam stopped herself from suggesting it would be more correct to call it a pride. It was almost time to go back to work. She just had one more question.

"Why did you think I'd know anything about cat people?"

Jeff was the one who looked surprised now. "You're always reading those books with covers that have spaceships or girls in armor on them and stuff. I figured if anyone I knew would know if Billy was full of shit, it'd be you."

"I think Billy might be full of shit," said Sam.

Jeff looked crushed.

SAM *DID* ENJOY BOOKS WITH SPACE SHIPS and girls in armor on the covers, and due to that, in part at least, she knew people who might be more likely to know about such things than she was.

"Cat people? Like—"

Sam cut Whitney off immediately. "No, not cat people like anything. *Actual cat people.* At Rocky Flats, roaming the plains in packs. Um, prides."

"I haven't heard anything about that." Whitney was basically a one-stop shop for conspiracy theories, everything from Chapstick being a money-making scheme to make your lips *more* chapped to the Mandela Effect to the phantom time hypothesis—a favorite of local crazies, according to Whitney, likely due to the proximity of the National Institute of Science and Technology.

Whitney punched a few things into her phone. "Huh, that's intriguing…"

"What?" Sam fought against the urge to look.

"There's just zero information online about cat people at Rocky Flats."

"Why would there be?"

"Because basically anything you can think up is online already," said Whitney. "Rule 34 is just an uncomfortable manifestation of the Jungian collective unconscious, after all. Thus, the utter absence of anything that resonates with the search string 'cat people rocky flats' is practically proof that they're there."

Sam stared at Whitney.

"I'm not sure…"

"We should go check it out," said Whitney. "What are you doing tomorrow?"

Sam got out her own phone and checked her calendar. "Uh, not much…"

"Let's go, then. Early. Pack for a hike."

"It's supposed to snow…"

"It won't," said Whitney.

It did. Not a lot, but enough to be demotivating. For Sam, at least—Whitney was ecstatic.

"Isn't this great?" she said, when Sam opened the door of her Subaru and slid into the passenger's seat, keeping her heels outside.

"Is it?" Sam knocked the snow off her boots and then closed the door.

Whitney tapped the side of her nose as she threw her hatchback into gear. "Tracks!"

Sam mulled over the idea of *tracks* as they slipped and slid their way south on 119, and mulled over the idea of someone—some federal agency perhaps?—scrubbing "cat people rocky flats" from the internet as they cut over onto 93 to eventually wind around and hit the East Entrance.

All her life, Sam had eagerly read books where people heard about something weird and decided to go and see what was up with it. As it turned out, adventures were better when she wasn't the one having them.

"Okay," said Whitney, when they'd parked. From her CamelBak, she withdrew what appeared, in the yellowed murk of her car's overhead light, to be a hand-drawn map. "The forbidden Department of Energy area is due east of us. We'll just keep walking until we hit the barbed wire fence. I have clippers with me, don't worry." That wasn't why Sam was worried. "I don't think the fence is electrified, but I couldn't find confirmation of that, so we'll just have to use our discretion. I insulated my wire cutters, and hopefully we can find a big rock to put on the fence if it seems too sketchy."

Sam continued to say nothing—she hadn't known the area in question had been fenced off so thoroughly, which made her doubt Jeff's friend Billy had really been there. Why go to so much trouble to fish in a potentially plutonium-contaminated stream, when there were plenty of rivers and reservoirs without such associated difficulties?

"I watched a few YouTube videos last night on how to do all this stuff," said Whitney, taking Sam's hand and squeezing it. "We'll be fine."

"Great," said Sam, trying to muster some enthusiasm for her friend's sake. "Shall we?"

It started to snow again.

Hiking was actually pretty nice. Other than the wet crunch of their boots it was perfectly quiet, and it wasn't snowing too heavily. Not yet, at any rate. Sam hadn't checked her app to see if this was the last of it or the start of it. She didn't want to demoralize herself further, especially after they abandoned the trail for the rougher terrain surrounding the forbidden Department of Energy site.

"So," said Sam, after about an hour, when the silence had begun to wear on her, "do you think cat people would be people who have powers over cats? Or would cat people be like, half-person, half-cat?"

"Half-person, half-cat," said Whitney, immediately, and with confidence.

Sam nodded in agreement. "I think so to. So would "half" make them *more* or *less* catlike than the Thundercats? I'm thinking more."

"I feel like the Thundercats were barely one-third cat," agreed Whitney. "Except for Snarf."

"Yeah," said Sam. "I never knew what was up with that guy. I always found him disturbing, like, he's sort of the equivalent of a talking ape among humans, I guess? Since he's broadly similar in his biology, but less evolved…?"

"Do you think humanity would be capable of tolerating something like talking apes? I feel like we would have long ago wiped them out."

"That's dark," said Sam. "But you're probably right. You know what else is dark? As a kid, I got this book out of the library that was all about cats, and I learned that boy cats have like, dick spines? They hurt the female during mating, and I remember wondering if the Thundercats also had—"

Sam stopped at the same time Whitney did, because right there in front of them was the impression of a large paw. Possibly a cat's paw; Sam didn't know.

It was as big as her hand.

The snow was falling more heavily now, but only a few flakes had settled in the depression. Whatever had left it had been there recently.

Sam locked eyes with Whitney, and they both started looking around. Rocky Flats was pretty, well, *flat*, but there were hollows where something might leap out with the intent to ambush.

Behind them was another paw print. Also fresh.

"Run," said Whitney.

Sam agreed with her legs. As they sprinted back the way they'd come, Sam thought over the conversation that had gotten her here. In retrospect, she really should have asked what Billy had seen the cat people hunting.

RELICS

ELIZABETH RAYNE

Almost every single test result for the mummy had come back inconclusive.

Mallory and his team could just barely confirm human DNA. The desiccated corpse had materialized in the antiquities backroom of the museum one morning, not even tagged for study, wearing a strange hooded shroud with the hood pulled over its sunken face. Skin clung to defleshed bones. Glyphs tattooed all over its body taunted him in an indecipherable tongue.

"Computers only know what we program their brains with." Mark Caldwell gazed at the glyphs on the body that now went by the ID code LX492. "If it's some kind of weird out-there shit no one's ever seen before, we're screwed."

Caldwell was the last colleague who lingered in the backroom with the dust, the mummies and Mallory almost an hour after the museum officially closed for guests. Whatever language was inked on this body was nothing like the Egyptian and Mayan hieroglyphs he was used to. The only thing that even came close was a curious tattoo on the inside of Mallory's left wrist. When Caldwell asked about it, the professor had somewhat nervously brushed it off as an afterthought of his first Guatemalan dig and too many shots of Quetzalteca.

As Mallory lifted the mummy's arm, lab coat sleeves pushed to his elbows, the tattoo was exposed enough for Caldwell to inspect it again. Caldwell could have sworn the primitive glyphs were eerily close to a sequence he had seen somewhere on the body. He strained to remember, but a blast from the ancient and erratic air conditioner forced the professor's sleeves down.

"Go home, Caldwell," the professor muttered without lifting his glazed-over eyes from the mummy.

After the door clicked shut and the echoes of Caldwell's footsteps vanished into the bowels of the museum, Mallory glanced at the glyphs again and began to roll up his left sleeve.

Mallory finally locked the exam room three hours later and took the shortcut out the back door. He gasped in the suffocating humidity of the New Orleans summer, whose heady jasmine and gardenia perfume never really masked the swampy miasma rising behind the museum. An odd greenish light flickered in the corner of his eye like a stray firefly. Something was pulling him through the biting haze of mosquitoes and downwards toward the swamp.

Bioluminescent water glowed under a canopy of mangrove branches. Warped faces, humanoid and fe-male, rose from its lurid green waters and stared at him with eyes that flashed almost neon. Their skin was an acid dream of oilslick rainbows that mesmerized him into surrender.

We know what you seek. You seek an answer.

He felt a curious warmth pulsing through his veins. Colors seeped into his consciousness, the visible spectrum swirling with the infrared in ways he could not describe with human words.

He seeded the Earth. We are his children.

The colors coalesced into a primordial wasteland that oozed and bubbled with proto-life. Billions of years fast-forwarded in seconds, and embryonic things began to emerge from those pools, tentacled creatures, winged and wingless, with multiple eyes and mouths that uttered blasphemy before language was ever invented.

This is as it should have been.

Billions more years saw the creatures evolving more eyes and appendages, gills and organs that bloomed like coral polyps. Bizarre formations metamorphosed into cities whose twisted spires rose in the Precambrian darkness and endured through aeons that dawned and died.

He had dominion over the Earth until your kind appeared. You drove us deeper and deeper. Our cities vanished, and his throne was abandoned. Slowly he wakes from the death-sleep. We thrive, and we feed, and we shall reclaim what was ours. We leave behind a warning with the bones.

Mallory saw through a myriad of eyes, into gaping mouths oozing with digestive fluids that liquefied and consumed everything but the skin and bones. Glyphs twisted before his eyes. Ancient lines and curlicues danced with crude bipedal figures, and he suddenly understood the answers that had eluded the microscopes and machines.

We will reclaim this planet when he wakes. It has already begun.

One of the faces rose from the murk, and her form began slithering and twisting into a mass of protoplasm whose cephalopod head writhed with tentacles. Mallory no longer knew how to feel fear. His entire being was overwhelmed as he stared straight into the creature's single octopoid eye as its lamprey mouth opened and its tentacles entangled him. In the singularity of its pupil, he saw the cosmos as it was unnumbered light-years away, planets that spawned the creature's great-great-great-ancestors, stars being born out of fiery chasms and collapsing into supernova deaths.

"Left that damn mummy on the table again," Caldwell muttered when he opened the door the next morning.

He had barely slept during the night, plagued by alien dreams he only half-remembered. Fumbling with his Tutankhamun coffee cup, he pulled a rolling chair up to the exam table. Double espresso streaked the boy king's death mask.

As Caldwell set his coffee cup down near the sink behind him, he noticed something off about the archive drawers. Some intern must have left one open. Whoever it was had also left the back door open, because the sick green smell of the swamp had crept inside. He shuffled over to investigate. The same drawer the mummy was usually kept in overnight should have been empty, except there was a body inside, and its ID tag was LX492.

Caldwell was suddenly wide awake. He rushed to the table and found himself staring at the other mummy's exposed left wrist.

He had seen Mallory's tattoo enough times when the professor rolled up his lab coat sleeves, even with the air conditioning rattling away. For a moment, Caldwell wanted to believe the same glyphs just happened to be on the same wrist of this new unidentified mummy. The rotting vegetation of the swamp was now invading his nostrils. He sucked in a breath and pulled back the hood of the shroud.

Even as obscured as it was by glyphs, the face was unmistakable.

Caldwell knew he was staring into the sunken eye sockets of what remained of Professor Richard H. Mallory, whose last expression among the living had been a euphoric smile.

Caldwell's dreams came rushing back as his vision melted into kaleidoscopic nebulas. He was surrounded by the bubbling

darkness of nascent Earth, from which amoebic organisms blossomed into mollusks and crinoids and fungus-things that had swarmed the planet before humans were even a figment of its imagination.

This is as it should have been.

As he finally heard the words he had been struggling so long to understand, Caldwell felt nothing but ecstasy as tentacles seized him and he hurtled into the cosmic void.

THAT BOOK

AVE ROSE

VERE AND CAT HAD ALWAYS BEEN AN ADVENTUROUS, EXPERIMENTAL COUPLE AND NOT JUST WITH FOOD, MUSIC, PLACES AND SEX. VERE WAS AN ANTHROPOLOGIST AND HISTORIAN. CAT WAS A CHEMIST AND BIOLOGIST. BOTH EXPERTS IN THEIR FIELDS, THEY WEREN'T YOUR TYPICAL ADRENALINE JUNKIES. THEY WERE OBSESSED WITH LEARNING, ANALYZING, EXPERIMENTING AND DOCUMENTING THE UNDISCOVERED. BUT UNLIKE OTHER PIONEERS OF SCIENCE, VERE AND CAT NEVER PUBLICLY SHARED THEIR FINDINGS.

They believed their most successful discoveries were obtained by combining mind altering substances with natural human activities. Their first experience was with Salvia, which they smoked while Vere was hard inside of Cat, as they became a seed that grew into vines that wrapped around the planet. They snorted Ketamine, then hopped onto a keytar flying through outer space, landed on a warm red planet and took a romantic walk on brick-colored sands of a solar beach. While Vere gave Cat cunnilingus on Moxy, he became a surge of light and she a crystal palace. Every lick was his refraction hitting her walls, creating rainbows.

On 2CB, the noise from the subway sounded like an orchestra playing at the Disney Concert

Hall. They tried to eat pizza on Acid but it tasted like candy, and although it was yummy, it just didn't seem right to eat a plate of candy for dinner. Right now, it must sound like a bunch of psychedelic drug trips happening in the heads of two weirdos. Yet, if these were all in their heads, how could these individuals be experiencing the same phenomena in the same ways? Both being of scientific minds, they'd already taken into account the power of suggestion. So on their first adventures, they would separate after a trip to write down their journey. Each time their written comparisons were so uncanny, they eventually ruled out that theory.

After Vere and Cat tried all naturally grown and artificially engineered mind-altering substances, they entered the realm of the occult, where they saw potions as an exciting, uncharted territory.

They began with a virgin's blood concoction from an ancient recipe they spent a small fortune obtaining. After preparing and ingesting strictly as directed, both became ten years younger for a week. They presumed the effects would continue as long as they could keep making the concoction, but they weren't interested in eternal youth, so it wasn't worth the trouble. Yes, dancing and mating as their younger selves was amusing, but nothing new.

When embarking on this journey, they didn't expect a literal result. They speculated the potion would induce some kind of regression, where they could experience each other as children. However, the discovery that folklore could produce a result that wasn't just mind-altering, but physically altering, changed everything. And now, these two were on a serious hunt for more.

Vere and Cat traveled the world, acquiring magic potion recipes and their obscure ingredients. Many of these escapades ended up fruitless, or not what they hoped for. One day deep in a cave in the Philippines, while searching for a rare root, they came upon that book. It was perfectly preserved within a large rock that fell and broke beside Cat. It was written in an ancient filipino Sanskrit called Baybayin that Vere was able to read. For the most part, it did appear to be a book of magic, but to their disappointment, it wasn't one with potions.

Vere and Cat never wasted time experimenting with spell books. Still, it was a magnificent artifact, so they took it back home. Being Filipino, Cat was jealous that Vere could read Baybayin and she couldn't, so he promised to teach her. Since Baybayin was based on Tagalog, Cat's native language, Vere knew she'd learn quickly.

Soon, they had lost interest in whatever potion they needed the root for, and were both focused on that book. Every page was breathtaking with colorful depictions of animals, including a human. Vere found a page with a spectacular feline and thought it a perfect place to begin Cat's lesson. During this lesson, the words of the incantation were spoken robotically and sporadically as Cat was learning. She caught on much faster than Vere expected, and after a few days, she was ready to read the entire spell aloud. She spoke the words, then morphed into an actual cat. Catherine was standing in front of Vere as a cat that was still her size. She meowed at first, but then took a moment and started to speak English. He grabbed that book and did the same to himself. They pummeled each other, spoke cat to one another, tried different foods, leaped around in the parks at night, and of course fucked like crazy.

In a matter of months, they went through that book entirely, changing themselves into every creature they could, and used the human spell to return to their original forms. They were fascinated and enthralled by the amount of empathy and understanding they gained from every creature they became. Surely, this was a magical and wonderful thing, so why did they still hunger for more? And for more of what?

At one point, Vere jokingly mentioned that he wanted to become a centaur. That's when Cat had an epiphany. She proposed to Vere that conceivably, they could create new spells, mixing the incantations from different creatures. Carefully, they started by mixing the horse incantation with the human one to become centaurs. It worked flawlessly.

So they went wild, turning themselves into whatever mythical creatures that book had the power to do, from merfolk to minotaurs, even venturing to non-human hybrids such as chimeras. As strange as it seems, this still was not the "more" these two were craving. There was an annoying common factor in all of these experiences. Though mythical, they were all creatures from earth. And since they had already transformed into every animal in that book, the hybrids only offered a remix of something they already felt. But what else could they do?

After years of experimenting with that book, they became quite good at it. They started to feel the power of every word, until they both came to the damning realization that the magic wasn't just in the incantations- it was in each word. Vere and Cat devised a plan to carefully select specific words from different spells in that book to create beings never described before, beings not of this earth, perhaps even not of this realm, to experience a physical phenomenon that would surpass the cosmic trips from their psychedelic adventures. Finally, after who knows how long...the words were chosen, the incantation was designed and they were ready. Vere and Cat chanted the spell together. And this time was different. As their physical bodies began to change, so did their surroundings, their thoughts, their souls. The two reached out towards each other as they began to lose what it felt like to be human, losing that connection to earth, that connection to one another.

Because these intrepid lovers were hell bent on experiencing something that did not exist in this world, they ultimately turned into that which could not exist in this world. So when their transformations were complete, Vere and Catherine vanished into the unknown. Their story with us stops here, because where they went and what they became could never be understood by any earthling mind.

MYTHS AND LEGENDS
by Kathe Koja

SO IT'S TEN-THIRTY, THERE'S NO MORE CHAI, AND "SYMON SAYS" IS A RERUN (THE ONE WHERE SYMON AND MICKEY GET STUCK IN THE GYNECOLOGIST'S OFFICE), SO I TURN TO THE KEYBOARD: BECAUSE I HAVE GOT TO WRITE THIS PAPER, THIS PLAY, FOR DRAMA, INTRODUCTION TO DRAMA, I NEVER ASKED TO BE INTRODUCED BUT MR. BANKS WAS SUPPOSED TO BE AN EASY GRADER. SO HERE I AM, TRYING TO PICK A TOPIC. THE PAPER'S DUE IN THE MORNING.

Write a one-act play (three pages, at least two characters) about one of the Myths or Legends on the topic list: Mermaid Summer, Thor vs. Loki, Leprechauns and Fairies, When Cupid Met Psyche.) "When Cupid Met Psyche"? Why not "Psycho Psyche," and she stabs Cupid through the shower curtain in the Olympus Motel? —Actually I didn't make that one up, Davy did. Davy's always saying stuff like that, he's really funny and really smart, so smart that half the time I don't even get his jokes but I laugh anyway so he won't think I'm a dumb blonde. Unless he thinks it anyway, but won't say so because he's so nice. And he's amazing-looking, too, did I mention that?

Ten–forty five. Is there really no more chai? No cold soda either? My brother probably drank it all, the slob.

Eleven o'clock. Myths and Legends. Fairy tales.

We have many names, we are everywhere, we have always been. Fire to your clay, we burn, rise as sparks while you stamp and slobber in the mud. We are the stuff of your desires, we grow wild. Wild. Every name you have for us is wrong.

MERMAID: Come with me into the sea.

FISHERMAN: But I can't swim. And I can't breathe underwater.

MERMAID: I'll breathe for you. Just come on.

FISHERMAN: But I don't even know your name.

MERMAID: That's OK. You can call me

…NO, THAT'S STUPID, I don't even like mermaids. What else is there? Leprechauns and fairies, gag. How could anyone believe in that stuff, I mean even in the Dark Ages or whatever people still had to have some common sense? Although according to Mr. Banks their fairies weren't like the Tooth Fairy and fluffy pink wings and all that. But it's like believing in, in ghosts or the Twilight Zone or something, the monster under the bed (or the basement, that's where mine used to be, between the washer and the dryer; when I was little I would never, I mean never go down there in the dark. My mom would ask me to bring up some soda or something, and I'd cry, and my dad or my little brother would have to go instead). How could anyone take that stuff seriously? Maybe I can write a comedy.

Peri, nökke, liosálfar, troll and droc and mazikeen. Blood-cousin to the fallen angels, the changeling spawn of exiled Adam forced, enticed, to lie with others than Eve; others than human. In those days there were giants in the land, does not the Scripture say so? Your Scripture. We have no written history, we need nothing but now, this breathing moment, our breathing in your ear; do you hear? Did you think it was the wind? An errant branch, a prowling animal?

Your paths are intersections for our travels, our dark sun rides another sky, but sometimes we pass close enough to see, to watch; to touch. Our touch is light, still it leaves a mark. Always it leaves a mark on the mud.

LEPRECHAUN: Always after my Lucky Charms! [He struggles but they hold him tightly. He's small anyway and can't get away.] Let me go!

GIRL: Hey don't have a stroke. We're going to let you go. In the myths and legends it says you give us three wishes, well we're not greedy, we just want one apiece. Right Davy?

GUY: Right. And I know what mine is right now. [Kisses GIRL.]

IN THE HALLWAY I hear my mom, saying something to my brother—"Lock the back door, Jamie?" and he just grunts back, nuh-nhug, too disgusting for human speech. Then her knock, tick-tick, her nails against my door; she has great nails, flawless, not all split and chipped like mine. A French manicure every other week, but will she pay for one for me? No. So unfair.

"Are you still up, Elise?"

No, I'm sleeping with my eyes open. "I'm doing homework."

"Oh. Well, don't stay up too late, all right? School starts early."

Door click, her footsteps down the hall. Now my room is lit only by computer light, like an aquarium, like the lights I used to have for my lizards. A glass box filled with green plants and flat grey rocks, when I'd pick up the lizards they'd squirm in my hand, then stop, turn to stone as if they knew there was nothing they could do but wait to be released again. I'd pet them, stroke their pebbly skin, bring them close to look into their eyes, black eyes as flat and otherworldly as, as what? Staring straight up into space, or down a well, you can't see to the bottom: as if they saw something, knew something I didn't, and were just waiting for me to see it, too. Or go away. Either way was fine with them.

[They put the leprechaun into a glass cage, like a big aquarium. He stomps and pushes at the walls, but he can't get out.]

LEPRECHAUN: My power can't work in a box! You have to set me free!

GIRL: We'll let you go as soon as you give us our wishes.

GUY: We want

—WELL, WHAT DO THEY WANT? How should I know? What would you wish for, I mean if it were really true, if there were such things as leprechauns or whatever? Not a million more wishes, that never works, or even regular stuff like tons of money or a new car (I'd probably pick a Jaguar, a silver Jag two-seater with burgundy seats). I mean those things would be nice, but—If you really had a wish, one you knew would be granted no matter what, what would you ask for? You'd have to want it a lot, and for always, not just now. And you'd have to be careful, because wishes can turn on you. Like that story we had in Lit last year, where the dead guy gets wished back to life, except he's not alive, he's like some horrible zombie even his own mother doesn't—"The Monkey's Paw," right. That must have been some monkey.

Maybe that's what I should write: "The Leprechaun's Curse," like where they wish for something but it gets all inverted and ugly, like the girl wishes they'd— No. I don't want to write that, I don't like to think about things like that.

But—but if it was a real leprechaun you captured in some aquarium, why would he, it, whatever, want to grant your wish? Even to get free? And even if he did, wouldn't he want a payback of some kind, revenge for getting caught in the first place?

What if the leprechaun knew what you wanted was bad for you, or just bad in itself, wrong, something that shouldn't happen? but he gave it to you anyway? Gave it to you because it was wrong? And then laughed when you let him go, jeered at you, like: Enjoy your Jag! And then you wreck and you're paralyzed? Or The one you want will love you always! Peering at you through the glass with flat eyes like my lizards', like black water in a well, like the sky at night that goes on forever, who knows how long that is? Do you really want to find out? And then he does love you, the guy you want, even when he's like a hundred years old and all sick and corroded and awful, even when he's dead, he stays with you.

Always.

You people of the mud, you dream of wishes granted, great gifts bestowed for nothing, as if to grasp must be to gain. Perhaps for you it is, with the simple toys you fancy, baubles like bubbles that burst when the wind rises. But still you are incorrigible, corruptible, you wish, you pray and we hear you, not the clean prayers of the will but the hot, wet, twisting whispers of the meat, the red heart that thinks itself the center of the sun; what sun? What heart? What you believe you want, we give, you get and then you scream, oh! Like a slaughtered beast: what a treat.

We answer your desire. Always.

GIRL: Let's let him go, Davy. It's wrong to keep him this way, cooped up in there like a lizard.

GUY: But what about our wish?

GIRL: We can make it come true ourselves, if we want to. [They kiss. The leprechaun, who's sleeping or something, hears them and wakes up. He puts his face against the glass, as if he doesn't believe what he's hearing.]

GUY: You're right, Elise. We'll take him back to where we found him and just let him go. OK? [He taps the glass.] You want to go back?

LEPRECHAUN [*smiles at them*]: No, let me go right here.

GUY: OK. [He puts out his hand but the GIRL grabs it back]

GIRL: No don't! What if it's a trick?

LEPRECHAUN [*still smiling*]: Why would I want to play a trick on two nice kids like you? Maybe I can grant your wish after all . . .

GIRL [*firmly*]: No thanks.

GUY: You're right again, Elise. [He picks up the aquarium cage.] Let's go, buddy.

CURTAIN

SO THEY TAKE HIM BACK to the woods, and let him go—and then what? Run back to their car, that's what I would do, run like hell and don't look back. And don't forget to wear your seatbelt on the way home.

That's the other thing that bugs me about these stories, you know? All these myths, the people in them are always like, Oh, ho-hum, I met a leprechaun today, like it's nothing. I mean, even if the leprechaun doesn't screw you over for life it's still pretty scary, don't you think? Just to meet a leprechaun, or even Cupid—he's got arrows, doesn't he?—to meet some kind of supernatural or extraterrestrial being, even if they don't do anything, that's scary. You're in the woods, gathering sticks or something, and then this bizarre creature crosses your path and even if you end up getting away OK it's still like, Hey, what just happened? And what if it happens again? Or something even worse? Wouldn't it make you, I don't know, kind of jumpy afterwards? Kind of terrified? Like you'd found out what things were really like, out there in the woods.

Twelve-fifty–four; I should stop now, I'm done anyway and I have to be up by six. In the kitchen, something makes a buzzy, thumpy sound: the refrigerator, turning off? Or on? Was it the refrigerator? Maybe it's my brother, come down for his fiftieth snack of the day. Or my mom, checking the back door again . . . My dad's in Sausalito, he won't be back tonight.

I yawn; my eyes are dry and I'm thirsty, really thirsty, for a soda or water or something. But then I'd have to go into the kitchen . . . What's wrong with going in the kitchen? Did I freak myself out with my own stupid play?

When I shut off the computer, my room will go dark, too. Aquarium light. I kept my lizards for a whole year, almost, but then they died. All at once, like they'd all decided that they were tired of living or something. I came home to feed them after school like I always did, and there they were, just lying there staring at me with their black eyes. I cried and cried, and my dad helped me bury them out by the fishpond.

But what nobody ever knew, what I never told anyone was when I saw them, in their glass box, I screamed. Not because they looked dead. Because they looked mad. At me.

WE ARE NOT EVIL, we of the fire; we are not good. We are: that is enough for you to know, mud heart, there in your hut, twig-house that could not withstand one-hundredth of our heat but we let you go, we have much to do and so little of it in your woods, your world, your blue sphere that rotates in this dark so great no one, not even we, can glimpse its end. We ride that dark, we gather what we need, we take what we deserve: our spoils: your dreams, your breathing infants, your courage in the night. Behind the air that wavers like glass our black eyes watch you: we grow wild in the wild places, and all places, now, are wild.

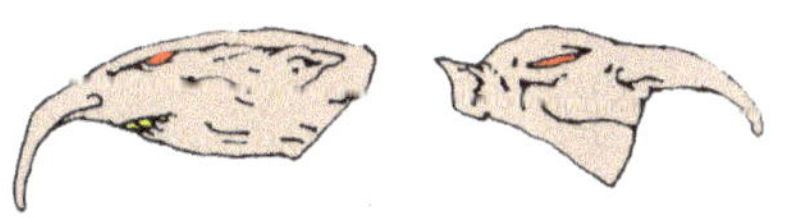

M

S.P. MISKOWSKI

FROM THE BACK SEAT I WATCH M GRIPPING THE STEERING WHEEL, NOT MOVING, CONSIDERING THE SITUATION. NOVEMBER ICE GLITTERS ON THE ROAD AHEAD OF OUR SEDAN, CAUGHT IN THE SHEEN OF HEADLIGHTS.

The man lies crumpled and shivering on asphalt. His breathing is a shallow wheeze.

One minute ago M slammed on the brakes, and my wooden horse went flying out of my hands into the windshield. It landed with a crunch at the same time the man hit the ground.

Framed by the rearview mirror, M's eyes have narrowed to pinpoints. On top of her head, and mine, damp hair is coiled around fat rollers with nylon bristles, held in stony compliance by metal pins and green silk scarves.

M is Mother if anyone stops us, if anyone wants to know. Our story is the same every night: We've driven to a salon to have our hair shampooed and set. We're on our way home to eat macaroni and cheese with bacon for supper. These are normal things to do, in this place.

"Doing normal" is our specialty, M's and mine. We blend. It's why we're here. We've seldom been noticed. Well, a few times.

Bundled in a corduroy coat, M's habit is to work the brake and gas pedals with one foot on each. A cigarette dangles from her mouth, stained with orchid lipstick.

"We're flyin' now," she likes to say, over her shoulder. We travel like this everywhere, middle-aged woman at the wheel and diffident seven–year–old in the back seat.

"Is this normal?" she asked, on our first night. "Does this configuration seem right?"

"Yes," I assured her. "Children avoid their mothers, here. Don't you see how they run away at the shopping malls, screaming, with snot on their lips?"

We have an understanding now, "doing normal" until orders arrive and the real assignment begins.

The street we're on is famously tricky, divined half by instinct and half by repetition memory. Lamps tower overhead, broken, as derelict as the bare sycamores spreading wicked fingers at our passing car in the deep dark.

The man who came ambling across the street, out of nowhere (as they say), wore a gray suit and tie with a smart little trilby perched forward on his head. Maybe inebriated, or maybe not. Didn't notice the bulky station wagon rounding the corner. Didn't hear us coming, M and I. His senses were startled and sharpened when a wet tire skimmed the back of his leg.

The car halted with a shriek, rocking forward and back on its axles. The man froze. He turned toward us.

M set the brake and lumbered out of the car. She stood in the middle of the street, cold air buffeting her and the man, no one else in sight. The man's voice was a shivery squeal.

"What the *hell*? Look what you've *done!*" His hat was gone and the back of his shoe, the part protecting his little Achilles tendon, was smashed flat.

"You're all right," M said.

"You could've crippled me!" he shouted.

"It's only your *shoe*," she told him, the bulbous mass of her cranium beginning to writhe beneath the green silk. "I will pay for your shoe."

"*Are you crazy?*" he shouted. "You almost hit me! You should be *arrested!*"

"You're all right," she said again, her voice like water gliding over ice. I recognized the glimmer behind her eyes.

"You don't belong on the road! Where do you come from, you *maniac?*" He pulled off his broken shoe, aimed like he was going to throw it at her.

M drew up to partial height, until the corduroy coat hung about her shoulders like a floppy bolero. A quiver of movement shifted her scarf to one side.

"There's nothing wrong with you," she said. "Go to your home."

"What the hell?" the man stammered. "You freak—you—you—*bitch!*"

M strode back to the station wagon and climbed inside, folding to her "doing normal" size again. She checked the mirrors, made sure the man was squarely behind the car, shifted into reverse, and hit the gas pedal.

The screech of brakes accompanied my toy horse flying from my hands. I saw the man fall and turn to a pulpy mass on the road.

M sits silently pondering. The driver's door opens again.

Now the part that never gets old.

A flutter of wind catches M's scarf, tugging it down around her neck. The green and writhing membrane opens, flaring from her facial bones like enormous wings. Flickering tongues emerge, naked, alive, and hungry. The run-over man greets the sight with screams until the membrane envelops his broken flesh with soft murmurs of digestive fluid: Mmmmmmmmmmmmmmm.

From the trees something normal, deprived of a meal, takes wing and flies away.

ALL THAT CREEPETH
STEFANIE ELRICK

ISA HAD SLEPT ROUGH PLENTY IN HER LIFETIME, BUT THE ROOT-TWISTED JUNGLE EARTH JUST WOULDN'T KEEP STILL BENEATH HER. WHEN SHE CLOSED HER EYES, SHE KNEW IT WAS MOVING, ENTWINING MUSCULARLY, LIKE A BED OF NESTING SERPENTS.

She needed to pee again and stretched out her back, but they'd been warned not to stray too far. Their fire threw a diminishing perimeter round the campsite: a circle to ward off roaming creatures in the night.

Pulling on her boots and picking up her flashlight, she hoisted herself up and prepared for the insect-ridden pitch. Hooting, hissing, shrieking; for once, outside was noisier than inside her head. Occasionally, an obstinate star cluster penetrated the kapok and ramon trees, but heaven's light barely made a dint down here.

Squatting, she held her breath and tried to relax, coaxing stress-taut muscles to expand and release. A gush, before a crackling from the fire's heart, then shuddering as if the earth turned over in its sleep. A spasm; something pinching at her rump flesh, burnt-orange and pus-yellow in the glare of her torch. A huge critter's body curled protectively around a clump of its young, with articulated joints and vicious, crescent-moon legs.

"Ciempies," a nameless relative informed her in their native tongue. Another added, "See how quickly she defends herself? How fiercely she protects all her babies from harm?" Isa nodded, straightening with a series of cracks and clicks, noting the totem amongst a growing list of signs.

THE NEXT MORNING, a livid red lump had formed, her glands were swollen and her skin felt two sizes too small. Brayan, their shamanic guide, rubbed on a greasy ointment, shaking his head when she mentioned tonight's opening ceremony.

"Drinking now would be too dangerous."

"But I am strong, I need to purge." *And we have nothing left to lose,* her spirit-chorus added.

His eyes betrayed his lingering doubts. Back in Iquitos, she had to convince him that she wouldn't slow them down. He saw an old woman, a burden, a problem, and knew nothing of what she'd already survived: the rootless childhood, the violent lovers, the maniac doctors—this world's relentless psychic dismembering.

"The jungle has its ways. I will send for someone to take you back. It isn't fatal, but I'm worried about your heart."

Isa tightened, staying outwardly silent. Inside, her brethren cursed. Corbade, imposter, un sin alma! She would have her rebirth, or walk into the river and never look back.

THAT NIGHT, Brayan's ceremony rumbled through her flimsy plastic tent; drumming, retching and rattling alongside the cicadas and shivering leaves. Isa crept out to watch through the woven reed walls as her fellow travelers drank murky vials of bitter brew. They claimed to know suffering, these pampered tourists, but they'd never been squeezed by their system's iron fist. She'd only been sixteen when they'd labeled her 'schizophrenic.' At eighteen, they'd sterilized her womb.

The jungle has its ways. A new voice. Unfamiliar. Not of her clan, but compelling and leaden in its weight. Come, sweet daughter Isadora, into the dark where you can be seen.

Deep in the forest, the Amazon's fecund nocturnal ecology hummed its own ritual clamor. All screeching, slithering and burrowing things harmoniously bred, slept, killed or fed. In a clearing, an old woman waited, in the trunk of a hollowed-out tree.

"Why have you come?" An owl landed on her crooked back; her eyes glinted like fallen stars.

"They stole our future and dishonored our past; we have come to find our way back." Isa's mouth moved but she was merely a puppet, the last and final conduit of their resolute will.

"You ask for help?"

"We will do anything to find peace, Sachamama. We have suffered so much, and wish to find our way home."

"You are too bright for their world, my little mestizo. Come, lie in my arms, where you belong."

Grateful, Isa's body sank down, resting finally among the roots and cool, dank rot. The Jungle's song swelled as her mind slowed, each generation letting out a tender sigh. Isa watched as the Grandmother opened the bird's mouth, pulling out a wriggling talisman. With its fangs, forked antennae and armored body, this creature would never let itself be easy prey. Laying her blessing on Isa's stomach, she parted her knees and let the insect find its way.

Once inside, it would chew away her sedimentary hurt, heal centuries of suffering and numb every single wound. As it did, Isa's body would narrow and lengthen, her spine extend and skin harden into toughened plates. This time, nothing would ensnare her or threaten her babies, or chase her from her home. Now her kiss would be poison, and all that creepeth call her Queen.

ANNA TAMBOUR
WHO KNOWS
WHERE THE
WASP CAN
WEAR HER
STING

"NEXT, UH—" THE BORED HALIBUT ROLLED HIS EYES AT THE CEILING. "OH, WHY DON'T YOU HAVE PRONOUNCEABLE NAMES?"

"In her eye. Her piercing gaze," whispered Kate* (*the names have been changed) while tentatively rising from the window sill.

"In her retort," answered Petruchia.

They were playing "Who knows where?" to wile away the time while they were waiting, as well as to lessen the fear each had.

They'd never met before, both of them being loners. But the program enforced a degree of, if not friendliness, then enforced camaraderie due to them being assigned the same room. After all, their surgery and treatments were likely to be the same.

"How many did you do?" asked Kate.

"Only a hundred and fifty or so that have a chance, though I stocked them well. Those cuckoo wasps. I kept trying to lead them off my trail—"

"We can only try. Better luck next year."

"If we get one."

"We must think poss—"

"This way," said a naked mole rat crossly. The three flew through a maze of tunnels till the mole rat banged through a door and was gone in a scurry.

"Perch," said someone from behind a screen.

The two mud wasps looked around.

The room's walls were plastered with positivism. Before and After pictures of celebrities. All the Before pictures being, of course, of the dead—for whom life's way too short. There's the antechinus male who, like all his counterparts, fucked to death. And that brainiac houdiniac, the octopus who starved herself to death as she cared for the eggs she's laid.

It costs a fortune here to escape that fate. But with the power of positive thinking, and flexible terms, even you can afford a new lease of life from Flatworm Rest Longevity Center,

Kate had revealed the location of a field of genetically modified pansies, their companion flower-spiders having adjusted to suit. Petruchia had pointed out a forest where honeysuckle vines had made every tree into tentpoles. There were, therefore, lakes of nectar hanging from the trees.

Anyway, here they were, waiting in a room plastered with horror and hope. They'd perched as ordered, and each couldn't help picking up as many feet as possible. The perch was cold, alien metal.

"At Flatworm Longevity," said the still disembodied voice, "We believe in educating our guests fully about our treatments, products, and services in order to enhance your experience."

The voice came closer, as its owner emerged from behind the curtain.

"Our client consent forms provide valuable information about treatments you may be receiving," it said. It looked them over as if it doubted they had brains. "You have filled out the consent forms, have you not?"

"Don't you have them?" Kate blustered. "We've paid so much, we expected better service."

Nothing in the publicity had prepared Petruchia for this.

Granted, it's extraordinarily pushing things to ask to live a season longer than her own mother. And to ask to live 50 more seasons. That's unbelievable, but if you see the claims enough times, and if it costs so much . . .

But she'd been through so many stages in life already. She liked this body.

"Are you an After?" she blurted.

"Petruchia!**" (**remember: not her real name) hissed Kate. "You know you'll have to make some compromises."

Petruchia's wings clattered, but she had to know.

Those limp things hanging. Six limbs of assorted fantastical uselessness. It can no more fly than it can walk up, or hang. Or pounce! How could it, if it's a she, get spiders for her babies? And what's it holding in that useless clamp? A thorn? Maybe it thinks a thorn a good substitute for jaws, or maybe it can never eat again. She felt hungry for nectar. This thing might be like the mother octopus, forever. And where's the ovipositor? And where can this thing wear its sting? In their place, a wound dressing!

Petruchia remembered stories, tales she'd put out of her mind because she wanted oh, so much to live in this wonderful body for more than just one season.

"You were one of us, weren't you?" she asked.

"One of you?" the thing laughed. "Hardly."

A flapping knock at the doors got the thing up and answering. On the floor was that halibut receptionist. Those two eyes looked up accusingly.

"Haven't you processed them yet? You know all patients should be prepped within two hours."

"Almost ready," lied the thing, turning back to the two patients.

"Sorry," it said. "Halibuts are naturally testy, and that one's going through a mid-life crisis."

"How long do they live?" asked Kate.

"We didn't quite know before, and now we'll never know. But enough of that. You're both coming for the complete job."

"Excuse me," said Petruchia. "But you're clearly a success story. What were you before?"

Its face did something with that tiny hole it had instead of mandibles, which must have excited what looked like parasitic worms in two legs with useless appendages for climbing and perching.

"I was a shrew," it said. "Haven't they done a marvelous job? I admit the wasp waist is difficult to maintain, and I'm not so keen on the naked mole rat look, but aren't I beautiful? Now, to you."

Never did two wasps fly so fast and so far, though at the end of the trail, they'd reach Death.

Better that by far. That face! A blob with holes, two wet and glittery. And on her head, snail eyes on stalks.

And that waist? Only a shrew could think that, a waist.

Emma Alice Johnson
A CENTAURESS WALKS INTO A BATTLE

"**POUR ME SOMETHING THAT BURNS,**" THE CENTAURESS TOLD THE BARMAID WITH A WINK AS A BEARDED BEAST OF A MAN SCRAPED HIS BARSTOOL ACROSS THE PACKED DIRT FLOOR TO SIDLE UP BESIDE HER.

"A woman like you shouldn't be alone in a place like this." He blew the words through his bristles like spitting seeds, carrying the stink of rotting teeth with them.

Even if his eyes weren't fuzzy with drink, he couldn't have seen the set of her jaw through the smears of color she had painted on for this rare night out, nor the striations of her sleek muscles through the silken pink ruffles of finery that covered her torso and cascaded down her back, over the spot where human turned to horse, over her four rigid legs with their hooves planted firmly, steadily on the ground.

She grinned. "I suppose you will protect me?"

"Ask any man at this mangy inn and he will tell you there is no greater warrior in the land." He gestured grandly toward the drunken, disinterested patrons. "I've been battling since birth."

As a filly, she had followed her mother and father into battle. This was their life, and the life of the generations that had preceded them. It would be hers as well. They taught her to swing a sword, always for results, never for show. At great cost, they demonstrated the mistakes not to make, leaving pieces of themselves on the battlefield in the process, until one day, when there was no more of them left to walk away and she stood on the battlefield alone, a mare now, head held high, her muscles painted with the blood of her enemy.

The man slapped his formidable bicep with his opposite hand to emphasize the pink lines that crisscrossed it. "My scars tell all that need be told."

"I see."

To her, scars were nothing to brag about, a symbol of one's inability to defend oneself. Her skin remained pristine, untouched by blade. No cudgel had damaged her fur. She had no marks save for those on her hocks from charging too quickly into battle over jagged rocks or through bramble. They had only recently healed from her last fight, when she had nearly broken all four of her legs by hurling herself off a cliff to position herself in the middle of the fray. She had landed awkwardly on rough terrain, but recovered confidently with sword drawn, much to her enemy's slit-throat surprise.

"I have fought in many battles in my time," he said, tugging at his beard with gnarled fingers. "Hundreds of battles."

"Oh!" she said. The bartender slid a goblet of brown muck in front of her and she finished it in a single sip.

She had fought in fourteen battles. Granted, she was younger than this man, but she was certain those fourteen were all that had occurred in her lifetime within the radius her hooves could carry her. She had also been in thirty-three skirmishes, forty-nine one–on–ones and had once been ambushed by a sorceress with a trained bear. That one had been dicey, as she had never dealt with magic before and a whispered spell turned her horse body to stone temporarily. Thankfully, the bear had much greater allegiance to the half of a roasted pig the centauress carried in her sack than to the sorceress.

"I've broken blades over the skulls of marauders," the man continued, sipping carefully from his own mug for fear of spilling into the thickets of his beard.

She had left a sword behind only once, after slicing it deep into the craggy cheek of a festering cave troll, who took offense at the gesture and attempted to mash her underfoot. She had easily dodged his stomps. In his anger, he had neglected the cliff she guided him toward, and he stumbled over the edge, taking her blade with him. She had loved that sword. She still mourned for that sword.

"If anyone here so much as looks at you in an untoward manner…" He trailed off, tapping a forefinger on the pommel of the battleaxe he dragged alongside him.

She gazed at the man's fingers as they grasped the axe handle. They were thick, with sprouts of black hair twisting from gashes and spots of dry skin, not weak by any means. Sometimes, for fleeting moments, on the darkest of nights, she forgot her strength and longed to feel safe, to feel protected. If only that was something as easy to find as a macho man with a battleaxe. But then the sun would rise, and she would stretch her arms to the sky and dig her hooves in deep beside a battlefield red with her enemy's blood, feeling ashamed for wanting anything more than her own strength to see her through.

"I like you, woman of few words."

The man bought more rounds and told more tales. The two of them tapped their goblets together 'til dawn, when he finally crumpled drunk to the floor, squeezing his battleaxe against his chest like a toy.

The centauress drained her last drink, stepped over him with her powerful horse legs and walked out into the waiting, ever–warring world she called home.

IN OUR SHALLOWS WE ARE SMALL

MEHITOBEL WILSON

We who slip languid between the green-furred pillars built from thrown-down bones are livid with envy. We who made becalmed forests of alien refuse and cultivated in them our viscid, intoxicating flora still hunger for another world. We, our raw skin coated in the divine slimecoat that shields us from the blistering burn of the water and eases our passage through its clinging turbidity, are jealous. We are jealous.

We must wait.

Drunk on the fruits of our muculent garden, we rest in the still shallows, and dream of the Brinelands.

The dry-striders cooked the outer realms, we know this. The waters moved. Our lake settled over an immense stone building that had once belonged to the dry-striders. Beneath the rot on the lake bed our ancestors found hard, crumbling ribbons, and we understood that the striders had once used those to traverse their blasted lands. The wisest among us explained that the striders could not convey themselves rapidly in the spaces beyond the water for they had neither fins nor wings. The wisest among us taught us about chariots, and wheels.

Intoxicated and jealous, we drift. We starve, because we must wait. We rise and tip our faces, breaking through the foaming scum on the surface, and sip our air, and down again we sink.

The ancestors have told us of the Brinelands. We have but one stone building to shield us from the sun. They have thousands, and the thousands are gargantuan, level upon level of stone and iron and smooth glass. Here a thousand, there another, and again, another, ranging over incalculable distances, from the warm slow surfs to the colder, rockier waters. The cities beneath the waves house and protect an abundance of life, of food, of cool shade and fortifications. The ragged shards of city-top that stand above the water glitter with dried salt. On nights when the winds blow cool, if the moon is bright, the rooftops gleam with the wet churn of night-basking bodies.

Beyond the cities lie the depths.

I yearn for the depths so badly that it causes me pain.

I yearn for the darkness, for the expanse, for the dilution. In our shallows we are small, our putrid water betraying us. In the depths we can grow fat and giant, like the rest of them. The weight of the deep water will firm our flesh. The minerals will bolster our bones. The currents will buffet us, and we will let them toss our bodies about and we will feel joy, and then we will set our tails to the ready and ride the currents from city to city, and out into the beyond.

We will not eat them, our sea-kin.

Nor shall we seek to conquer them, for we are small, and so few.

Our hope is that they will welcome us.

The waiting must be finished soon. We hunger too intensely.

Before, the dry-striders slaughtered one another and rained their gutted dead upon our heads. We shredded the flesh from their giant bones and ate, and ate, and ate, but their bodies were foul and numerous. They bloated and burst and made our waters noxious.

We claimed their gems and admired their weapons. We delved into the garbage on the lake bed and made our own swords.

For a time, we killed each other, to see what it was like.

But we are too few, and the killing and devouring of one another would have emptied our lake, and we would never escape to the Brinelands.

The glut of corpses ceased at last, but we needed to eat, so we ventured to the edge of our lake and rose to the surface. Dry-dwellers crouched at the shoreline, pulling measures of our lake away and pouring the water into twisted contraptions, cawing hoarsely to one another now and then.

They saw us, thought we were distant, but we were just small. We are few, but we are enough. Together, we took them under, and fed.

Their meat was much different when fresh. Their blood was salty.

We took them often, until they stopped coming at all.

Some of us left our lake to hunt, but failed. Too small, too few.

But we knew about the Brinelands.

We knew about weapons.

We knew about wheels.

We waited.

And now, in the night, when the moon is high, a dry one comes to our lake's edge. He has forgotten us, or dismissed us, or needs its portion of our water.

All of us together see him there, and know our wait is done.

We see the forth from the scumline and set upon the dry one, our swords at his pulsing throat, his rolling eyes, notched into the corners of his peeling lips. He reels and stumbles, barking harshly as our tails—they are weak and small and few, but together they are cruel enough—slap and slice him.

The translucent ropes we fashioned from harvested garbage pinch his flesh as we settle the harness around his shoulders. As we stab the knobs of his spine to prod him forward, he feels the full weight of us. He cranks his head around, blood drawn by our blades coursing from his mouth and sheeting from the black hollows under his eyes.

He beholds the rest of the lake folk crowded, triumphant, in our chariot of bone and some past world's refuse, our starved bodies robed in sodden long-fronded algae, and he caws and gibbers and stamps his feet.

None of his dry- striding brethren venture from the darkness to help him.

Now on the breeze comes the saline promise of the Brinelands, and we drive him toward it with the poisoned points of our swords. The fetid stench of our lake falls away behind us as our unlucky steed lumbers forth.

By sunrise, we will be at the oceanside. We shall breach the bounding waves, descend into the cities, and offer those fortunate denizens our swords. We shall grow as large and plump as the vast depths would have us grow. We shall join them, and be many.

Now, though, riding giddy upon this midnight strider, I turn my blade against his skin and allow myself just one little bite.

Or two.

WHEN SHE CAME, EVERYTHING FELL APART

by BETTY ROCKSTEADY

THE GAG MUFFLED THE MAD EMPRESS' MOANS, THE CRYPTIC INTONATIONS OF HER SPELL LOST BENEATH THE MURMUR OF THE CROWD. THE GUY FUCKING HER WASN'T GOING TO LAST MUCH LONGER. HIS SWEAT DRIBBLED A RIVER DOWN THE CURVE OF HER BACK, INCHES BENEATH THE RAZOR WIRE BINDING HER HANDS.

I was close enough to see his balls clench tighter as he lost himself in her, to hear his grunts of pleasure turn to bliss, and close enough to be splattered with blood when his body finally sagged and he fell away from her. The hole where his cock had been was deep, leaking unrecognizable fluids.

She would never be satisfied, no matter how many bodies piled up beside her.

We had summoned her, fucking fools that we were, after our women had slit neat slivers down their tongues and taught themselves to speak. The elders had promised us an Empress to restore order, but instead they had raised this wicked thing. The Empress! Ha! We offered her release and she enslaved us, sewed our women deep into the earth and demanded satisfaction. But the bitch would never be satisfied.

The binding, the gag—pathetic, ineffectual. It wasn't in her hands or her mouth that her strength lay.

She turned to me, splayed her legs wide, showed me the secrets of her universe. I thought of my wife, or tried to, but the scent of the Empress' sex overwhelmed me. Despite my revulsion, my cock hardened. The crowd behind me rustled again. I stepped forward, staked my claim. There were only moments to plug her up before the pain started.

She reared up on all fours like an animal, displayed herself to me. Her labia were engorged, dripping sweet fluids. I stroked her ass and beneath the rusted blood, her skin was smooth. My anger disappeared. Her hips moved and their gyratory language called me. She needed me. She needed me now.

I pushed her face into the dirt and pressed my shaft against her soft folds. Someone was saying something, someone was screaming at my side, but it was too late. I was hers.

Hands pattered against my back but I pushed them away, words I didn't understand, couldn't listen to, and then the gut-wrenching pain as I was pulled away. Rage filled my head, my vision blurred, I wasn't me, I was all heat of anger and flashes of red. I swung and a figure crumpled.

I would have hit him again, but instead I stumbled and ended up beside him on the ground. I saw his face and the anger subsided. Kabruss. My friend. Although he had aged tremendously in just days of this torture, I recognized the look in his eye.

"I have an idea," he said.

She would not wait. She had no time for conversation. The cacophony of another universe screamed and when it did, my cock hardened, larger than ever before, past desire, ready to burst, and I turned back but some other sap was ready to take my place and he filled her and the agony ceased.

Kabruss pulled me further away from the rutting grounds, into the sands. The crowd tapered out quickly. Days ago it would have taken hours to get through. How long now before she wiped us completely from the planet and we left her alone, forever, writhing in our dirt, screaming for release?

"Where are we going?"

"We're doing our own ritual."

"What do you know about rituals?" But I let him lead me, and as we left behind the last of the men, I saw Kabruss' brother, Brulio, a few yards ahead. Waiting.

"I know what we need to know. The constellation is still open. We have the power of three. And we have the intent." Kabruss' eyes rolled, showed too much of the whites. "It's all in the intent. That's where the elders fucked up." His hands moved like birds. "Do you think she's the only one of those out there? I saw when it opened. There were more." He leaned closer to me, his breath like spoiled milk. "I know what they did wrong. You see it too. You see what she wants! We've got something powerful right here." He grabbed his dick. "They never shoulda killed that girl. That's not what they want. We give them what they want and this time we'll get a real god—"

We approached Brulio. His expression was unreadable.

"Are you buying this?" I asked him.

"We've got days, man, and then we're all gonna be dead."

We passed into a circle of torches, and Kabruss' eyes flickered with their flame. Rudimentary, not the way the elders would do it, but it was something. The constellations were still right.

It was possible.

Kabruss peeled his pants off. I had never seen him naked before, never even imagined it. His penis was massive, and nearly twice as thick as mine. I had never thought of him, or any man, like that before, but he met my eye as his hand lowered and I felt myself stiffen in response.

"What do we do?"

"We curse that bitch." He spat in his hand, worked his cock harder. "We bring something else forth."

Brulio stood beside me, his hand moving with frenetic enthusiasm beneath his underwear. I caught her distant scent on the air and grew even stiffer. The earth beneath my feet pulsed.

"Picture him," Kabruss grunted, "Picture what we want to raise. Something to satisfy the bitch that can't be satisfied. Take our cum. Send us a god to tame the whore."

I stroked my cock and it came to life in my hand. The sun blazed on my back, my own sticky sweat lubricating my motions. I tried to picture a god to save us. I tried to think of my wife, of her body moving beneath me. I could only think of The Mad Empress, and the figure-eights her hips made as she pushed against me. These days of constant arousal had taken their toll and I couldn't hold back. Thick ropes of cum spurted from my cock, into the sands, and my dick *moved* in my hand.

"Sacrifice" the sun hissed and we whispered *yes, save us* and a powerful nausea brought me to my knees. My cock stretched and moved in a way I had never felt before, and when I looked down, two beady eyes looked back, a sliver of a tongue, and then razor sharp teeth *hot hot hot pain pain pain* and blood soaked the ground.

Weakly, I pressed my hand against the wound. Three snakes slithered away from us, and *something* opened.

First a hand appeared, then another, and a creature made of curves and steel pulled herself forth. Kabruss moaned next to me, fell to his knees, seeping juices into the earth. The blazing creature parted her thighs and our snakes streamed up into her cunt and disappeared inside her.

"No!" He bellowed, "No more women! We sacrificed! We did what you said!" This last ditch effort was a failure. Our dicks were failures.

She sniffed the air, listened to the distant sound of moans, gazed past us to where the Empress writhed in the midst of the bodies of our brothers, moaning and pumping her hips into the air. This new creature's body gleamed, mirrored my face back to me, and I didn't recognize it at all. Her voice was liquid metal in my brain *Have any of you idiots even tried to make her come?*

"Yes! So many of us have died! So many of us have fucked her, but—"

No, she licked her lips with the tongue of a snake, *I asked, have any of you—*

Kabruss leaped forward. I had an insane moment where I thought it would work, that he would overpower her somehow, but the snakes dribbled from her mouth, one, two, three. Our snakes. But they had undergone some transformation as they squirmed their way through her body and they were *hungry.* They swarmed Kabruss, burrowed into his skull, and his screams ended but their sounds didn't stop, that terrible squishing as they worked their way through his meat.

The metal queen watched us. Considered us. Terror kept my tongue thick in my throat.

Your sacrifice is accepted.

The Mad Empress approached on bloody knees, stumbling through the sands. Our new metal queen went to her, and there was laughter and joy in their greeting. Gleaming silver embraced filthy flesh. Our creature untied the Empress' binds and removed her gag, cupped her face and kissed her mouth. Something bled out onto the earth, and they fell to the ground, bodies moving together. The mirrors reflected me again as she knelt between the Empress' legs, kissed thighs, and buried her face in her sex.

I let myself fall to my knees. Blood dripped beneath me. Brulio was still standing, his face glazed. I crawled to Kabruss. To what was left of him. The snakes squirmed through flesh and bone, worked his mouth, and he spoke in a voice I had never heard before "She's coming."

The sun exploded, the constellations fell down around us. The earth erupted, and our women crawled out, tangled hair strewn down their backs, their bodies and eyes glowing with something new.

I was too weak to look for my wife, but she found me. Her eyes were cold. She held my head in her hands, and I pushed her skirt aside, and as the lifeblood dribbled out of me, I kissed her where it counted.

CONJURE, GREEN GODDESS

Anya Martin

K'gor stands back, tanned and mighty, his jeweled dagger earned in battle and clutched in his bronze left hand, F'rithz's leash in his right. But the deep and inconsolable sorrow of Aelithra, Jene-Daiesh of Qu'dun, is harder for him to bear than facing the fierce and merciless R'dath. Last night she had time for both lover and pet, but today she has no time even for her long beloved F'rithz. Sensing his mistress's deep distress and desolation, F'rithz lies quietly, bends its long ears back, and twitches its long tail in mutual anguish.

From what world the R'dath have come and why they choose to conquer Qu'dun, no one knows, not even the soothsayers in the high cliffs of N'ralingur. No prophesy foretold their arrival in starships bigger than the Qu'ree have ever seen with weapons that vanish an entire village in a flash of light. They have slain so many dear to Aelithra, for every one of the Qu'ree is dear to her. She is the Mother of all Qu'ree, and each death is like the death of her child, though the seeded egg that shall hatch to be her daughter nestles but for a few hours in womb darkness, not to emerge for many moons to first starlight.

The very survival of the Qu'ree lies at stake unimagined, not even in the dark days of the Il-lyrthirym. Their own starships, tiny compared to those of the R'dath, yet hover and whiz among the tall towers of the mountain city of N'ravdor, known for its legendary beauty. But the knowledge of the savage attacks and that the R'dath are on their way means every star captain weighs whether to stay and fight with little chance of success and almost certain death, or flee and hope to find another home-world, ever realizing the R'dath one day may discover and conquer it as well.

Every star captain, but K'gor, the handsome, long-haired barbarian, knows his place will always be fighting for the Jene-Daiesh. K'gor admires Aelithra not only for her beauty but also her great resolve in the face of what others see as sheer hopelessness. He has confessed his undying love for her and she to him, but their secret coupling last night, barbarian and Daiesh, has always been forbidden, and the knowledge that he carries its fruit, her daughter, cannot be said aloud. He is not Qu'ree, but the last of the H'rakk and never knew the father who bore him into the starlight nor the mother who seeded him. Their daughter will be something new and unknown. That is, if he lives long enough to hatch her.

Aelithra must banish all memories of their forbidden passion today. The one and only hope left for Qu'dun is the Living Oracle of the Green Water.

Standing tall on her hooves, Aelithra clasps the effigy of the great green god Gr'zrl, which with her hands, she has so carefully wrapped with vines from the Garden of Destiny. She steps back when the Living Oracle splashes an arched wave towards her as if hungry to accept the sacred offering. She knows the Green Water burns flesh, having seen She who was her own Mother consumed in the sacred basin—skin, hooves, and bone melting to join with the eternal flow of the Living Oracle. One day this fate would have also been her own, so that a sweet Qu'ree daughter could carry forth the role of Jene-Daiesh. But the coming of the R'dath has transformed all destiny and her daughter's father is not Qu'ree. The Green Water will never taste her nor her progeny.

Yet if the R'dath destroy all the Qu'ree, no need for Jene-Daiesh remains on Qu'dun and who should care?

Truly no one knows what the Living Oracle will reveal once Aelithra throws within the basin the divine effigy of Gr'zrl gifted by her ancestral Mothers for just such a desperate time. When the offering summons Gr'zrl from the depths beneath the city, will the Great Goddess devour only the R'dath or all that remains of Qu'dun?

The tellers warn that Gr'zrl's hunger aches beyond all hungers. Ancient beyond reckoning when slimy life first crawled onto the rocks from a primordial sea that births life on all worlds that hold life, Gr'zrl sleeps deep, deep below N'ravdor, the priestesses say. She sleeps until the day when the Oracle receives the effigy, and the ancestral Mothers warned that she will expect a sacrifice of a volume that matches the reason why She has been summoned.

Yet what other choice remains for Aelithra to save her people, her city, her world? Qu'dun is Gr'zrl's world, too, so perhaps the Goddess will not extract the most terrible of costs to save it.

She hopes the life of a Jene-Daiesh of Qu'dun will suffice.

For her world and her people, she will gladly accept death and whatever eternal servitude of passion Gr'zrl compels, even if she must be the final Jene-Daiesh and a half-H'rakk daughter takes her place.

Surely if the Goddess finds her sacrifice sufficient, her people will forgive her unholy trespass and see a new way forward. She gazes back at her lover and knows he will make a fine Protector until their daughter reaches the sacred age.

CONTRIBUTORS

WEIRD GIRLS AND OTHER ANOMALIES
LISA MORTON is a screenwriter, author of non-fiction books, award-winning prose writer, and Halloween expert whose work was described by the American Library Association's **READERS' ADVISORY GUIDE TO HORROR** as "consistently dark, un-settling, and frightening". She began her career in Hollywood, co-writing the cult favorite **MEET THE HOLLOWHEADS** (on which she also served as Associate Producer), but soon made a successful transition into writing short works of horror. After appearing in dozens of anthologies and magazines, including T**HE MAMMOTH BOOK OF DRACULA, DARK DELICACIES, THE MUSEUM OF HORRORS,** and **CEMETERY DANCE** Magazine, in 2010 her first novel, **THE CASTLE OF LOS ANGELES,** was published to critical acclaim, appearing on numerous "Best of the Year" lists. She is a six-time winner of the Bram Stoker Award®, a recipient of the Black Quill Award, and winner of the 2012 Grand Prize from the Halloween Book Festival. A lifelong Californian, she lives in North Hills, California, and can be found online at www.lisamorton.com.

CONJURE GREEN GODDESS
ANYA MARTIN'S debut collection, **SLEEPING WITH THE MONSTER,** is available from Lethe Press. Her novella **GRASS,** illustrated by Jeanne D'Angelo, was a Dim Shores limited edition chapbook, and her play **PASSAGE TO THE DREAMTIME,** illustrated by Kim Bo Jung, was published by Dunhams Manor Press. When not writing fiction, she's a journalist, editor/blogger-in-chief of *ATLRetro.com*, and co-producer, with host Scott Nicolay, of The Outer Dark podcast, which features interviews with contemporary Weird fiction and spec-lit authors, on This Is Horror network. Find out more at www.anyamartin.com and on Twitter at @anya99.

WHO KNOWS WHERE THE WASP CAN WEAR HER STING
ANNA TAMBOUR If you liked this story, Anna Tambour recommends (though she does even if you thought her story wasp-poo) these anthologies coming out later in 2019: **THE WEIRD FICTION REVIEW, UNCERTAINTIES,** and **D THE UNQUIET DREAMER.** Her latest books are the 2017 novel **SMOKE PAPER MIRRORS** and the 2018 collection THE ROAD TO NEOZON.

PUBLISHER
ODDNESS (author, publisher, producer) originates from unknown lands, and dabbles in modular synths and playing video games.

WHEN SHE CAME, EVERYTHING FELL APART
BETTY ROCKSTEADY is an eclectic author and illustrator from Canada. Her early exposure to Stephen King, The Weekly World News, and EC horror comics shaped her into the woman she is today. With art and fiction, she explores personal fears and resonances. Her debut novella, **ARACHNOPHILE**, is part of this year's Eraserhead Press' New Bizarro Author Series.

M
S.P. MISKOWSKI'S stories have appeared in numerous magazines and anthologies including T**HE MADNESS OF DR. CALIG-ARI, DARKER COMPANIONS: CELEBRATING 50 YEARS OF RAMSEY CAMPBELL,** and **THE BEST HORROR OF THE YEAR VOL-UME TEN**. Her books are available from JournalStone/Trepidatio and Omnium Gatherum.

A JUDGMENT MADE CAN NEVER BEND
MOLLY TANZER is the British Fantasy and Wonderland Book Award-nominated author of **CREATURES OF WILL** and **TEMPER** and the forthcoming **CREATURES OF WANT AND RUIN**, as well as the weird western **VERMILION**, among other titles. She is also the co-editor of **MIXED UP: COCKTAIL RECIPES** (and Flash Fiction) for the **DISCERNING DRINKER** (and Reader). For more information about her critically acclaimed novels and short fiction, visit her website, mollytanzer.com.

ALL THAT CREEPETH
STEFANIE ELRICK is a writer, artist and performer from Manchester, UK. As a performance artist she's blood-lined love poetry onto her body during 'Written in Skin' www.writteninskin.com and been strapped to a 12ft spinning timepiece for 'KAIROS' *www.kairosophy.com*. Things are just starting to get interesting at www.stefanieelrick.com

THAT BOOK
AVE ROSE is an LA based artist, automaton maker, jewelry designer, author and opera singer. She has written three books in the horror genre. Her visual work has been featured in music videos, TV shows, storefront installations, art galleries and museums around the world.

IN OUR SHALLOWS WE ARE SMALL
MEHITOBEL WILSON has been publishing horror fiction since 1998. She has been a Bram Stoker Award nominee, and many of her stories have been granted Honorable Mentions in the Year's Best Fantasy and Horror series. Recent stories appear in **APEX MAGAZINE, DEEP CUTS, NECRO FILES, ZOMBIES: ENCOUNTERS WITH THE HUNGRY DEAD, PSYCHOS,** and **SINS OF THE SIRENS**. Selected stories have been collected in **DANGEROUS RED**. Her newest book, **LAST NIGHT AT THE BLUE ALICE**, is an original novella from Bedlam Press.

MYTHS & LEGENDS
KATHE KOJA is a novelist, playwright, director and independent producer. Her work crosses and combines and plays with genres, from YA to contemporary to historical to horror. Her novels—including **THE CIPHER, SKIN, BUDDHA BOY, TALK, HEADLONG,** and the **UNDER THE POPPY** trilogy—have won awards, been multiply translated, and optioned for film and performance. She creates immersive performance events, solo and with a collaborative ensemble of artists, dancers, and musicians. She's globally minded, and based in Detroit USA.

ALWAYS A BRIDE
JESSICA MCHUGH is a novelist and internationally produced playwright running amok in the fields of horror, sci-fi, young adult, and wherever else her peculiar mind leads. She's had twenty-one books published in nine years, including her bizarro romp, **THE GREEN KANGAROOS**, her Post Mortem Press bestseller, **RABBITS IN THE GARDEN**, and her YA series, **THE DARLA DECKER DIARIES.** More information on her published and forthcoming fiction can be found at JessicaMcHughBooks.com.

A CENTAURESS WALKS INTO A BATTLE
EMMA ALICE JOHNSON writes stories and books and zines. She lifts weights and eats ice cream. If she could make out with any character from Greek mythology, it would be the minotaur. She lives in Minneapolis by the lakes.

RELICS
ELIZABETH RAYNE is an author and artist who writes for *SYFY Wire* and lurks around New York City.

ARTWORK
MIKE DUBISCH is an internationally known fantasy illustrator and graphic novelist. His art has been used in toy design and illustration for Star Wars and Dungeons & Dragons role playing games, covers for Aliens VS Predator, the graphic adaptation of Edgar Rice Burroughs' I AM A BARBARIAN, as well as appearances in the magazines SCIENCE FICTION AGE, REALMS OF FANTASY, THE H.P. LOVECRAFT MAGAZINE of HORROR, FORBIDDEN FUTURES, and THE CREEPS.

UNCLE KRUST'S GUIDE TO GUYS
CODY GOODFELLOW has written eight novels. His latest are **UNAMERICA** (King Shot Press) and **SCUM OF THE EARTH** (Eraserhead Press). His first two collections, **SILENT WEAPONS FOR QUIET WARS** and **ALL-MONSTER ACTION**, received the Wonderland Book Award. As an actor, he has appeared in numerous short films, TV shows, music videos and commercials.

9 781960 213112